Dear Parent:

Congratulations! Your child is taking the first steps on an exciting journey. The destination? Independent reading!

STEP INTO READING® will help your child get there. The program offers five steps to reading success. Each step includes fun stories and colorful art. There are also Step into Reading Sticker Books, Step into Reading Math Readers, Step into Reading Write-In Readers, Step into Reading Phonics Readers, and Step into Reading Phonics First Steps! Boxed Sets—a complete literacy program with something for every child.

Learning to Read, Step by Step!

Ready to Read   Preschool–Kindergarten
• big type and easy words • rhyme and rhythm • picture clues
For children who know the alphabet and are eager to begin reading.

Reading with Help   Preschool–Grade 1
• basic vocabulary • short sentences • simple stories
For children who recognize familiar words and sound out new words with help.

Reading on Your Own   Grades 1–3
• engaging characters • easy-to-follow plots • popular topics
For children who are ready to read on their own.

Reading Paragraphs   Grades 2–3
• challenging vocabulary • short paragraphs • exciting stories
For newly independent readers who read simple sentences with confidence.

Ready for Chapters   Grades 2–4
• chapters • longer paragraphs • full-color art
For children who want to take the plunge into chapter books but still like colorful pictures.

STEP INTO READING® is designed to give every child a successful reading experience. The grade levels are only guides. Children can progress through the steps at their own speed, developing confidence in their reading, no matter what their grade.

Remember, a lifetime love of reading starts with a single step!

www.stepintoreading.com

Educators and librarians, for a variety of teaching tools, visit us at www.randomhouse.com/teachers

Library of Congress Cataloging-in-Publication Data
Berenstain, Stan, 1923–
The Berenstain Bears by the sea / The Berenstains.
   p.   cm. — (Step into reading. A step 2 book)
SUMMARY: The Bear family goes to the beach, but before they can swim in the ocean there's a lot of work to be done.
ISBN 0-679-88719-9 (trade) — ISBN 0-679-98719-3 (lib. bdg.)
[1. Beaches—Fiction.   2. Bears—Fiction.   3. Stories in rhyme.]
I. Berenstain, Jan, 1923–   II. Title.   III. Series: Step into reading. Step 2 book.
PZ7.B4483   Bemkc   2003   [E]—dc21   2002013674

Printed in the United States of America   22 21

STEP INTO READING, RANDOM HOUSE, and the Random House colophon are registered trademarks of Random House, Inc.

The Berenstain Bears

BY THE SEA

The Berenstains

Random House 🏠 New York

Is it far,
Papa Bear?

Those seagulls mean
we'll soon be there.

There is the house
where we will stay.
Our shore vacation
starts today!

The wind was strong.
It opened the door.
Sand blew in
upon the floor!
This house was empty
for a while.
Each room has
its own sand pile.

Let's put on suits
and go in the water.

Not yet, son!
Not yet, daughter!

We must clean up,
room by room.
Here's a dustpan.
Here's a broom.

Now the clean-up
job is done.

It's time to have
some ocean fun.

Not just yet!
There's more to be done
before you start
your ocean fun.

There are

things to carry,

beds to make,

closets to clean,

walks to rake.

Mama, all of
that is done.
<u>Now</u> may we start
our ocean fun?

May we? May we?
May we, please,
dip our tootsies
in the seas?

Will you please relax!
You've got all day.
The ocean will
not go away.

There are many things
we must unpack.
Then we'll have
our little snack.

Mama, our little
snack is done.
Now may we start
our ocean fun?

Dears, it's much
too soon after food.

Rats and phooey!

Now, let's not be rude!

It's long after snacks.
May we go in soon?
It's getting late
in the afternoon!

That's why we're here,
to swim in the ocean.
But first, my dears,
let's put on some lotion.

At last we can go into the water!

Wait, my son!

Wait, my daughter!

But, Papa! Will we never
swim in the sea?

Relax! I just wanted you
to wait for me.

Come on, cubs!

Shake a leg!

Last one in
is a rotten egg!

The ocean is fun!
The ocean is great!
It may even have been
worth the wait!